My Little Bedtime Storybook Treasury

Published by Brimax,
A division of Autumn Publishing Limited
©2004 Autumn Publishing Limited
Appledram Barns, Chichester PO20 7EQ

Printed in China

Katie the Kitten   4
Penny the Pony   18
Three Little Ducklings   32
Cassie the Cow   46
Little Lost Chick   60
A New Friend   74
A Bucket for Dizzy   82
Visitors   94
The Birthday Party   104
New Shoes for Harriet   114
Mud   126
Atishoo!   136
Waves   152

Katie the Kitten

Katie the kitten was having fun playing with a big, bouncy ball. She chased it across the floor, under the chairs - and around the table.

Sam the dog watched as the ball spun across the floor towards him. THUMP! Bringing down one large paw, he stopped the ball!

"Meow! Meow!" cried Katie. "Stop it! That is my ball!"
"So it is," smiled Sam.

Katie decided to play upstairs with the ball, out of Sam's way.

She chased the big, bouncy ball over the rug, under the bed - and around some toys.

Teddy watched as the ball spun across the floor towards him. THUMP! Bringing down a paw, he stopped the ball!

"Meow! Meow!" cried Katie. "Stop it! That is my ball!"
"So it is," smiled Teddy.

Katie the kitten decided to play in the garden with the ball, out of Teddy's way.

She chased the big, bouncy ball over the grass, under the bushes and around the trees.

A bird watched as the ball spun across the grass towards him. Whoosh! Swooping down, he pecked at the ball!

"Meow! Meow!" cried Katie. "Stop it! That is my ball!"

"So it is," smiled the bird.

...9...

Katie the kitten chased the ball back indoors and into the kitchen.

BOING! BOING! BOING! The big, bouncy ball bounced across the kitchen floor and into her saucer. SPLASH! Poor Katie was covered in cold milk.

"Atishoo! Atishoo! Atishoo," said Katie. "Stop it, you naughty ball! I do not like being splashed with milk! Meow! Meow! Meow!"

The ball bounced out of the milk. Then it rolled past a spider and under the kitchen table.

"Please come back!" called Katie. "Meow! Meow!"

But the ball did not come back.

"The big, bouncy ball is very happy here with us!" said a little ladybird, flying down on to the ball.

"Then I shall leave it where it is," said Katie.

Katie decided to chase Sam the dog's tail instead of her ball.

"Woof! Woof!" said Sam. "Please leave my tail alone."

"I have lost my ball and now I am very sad," cried Katie. "Meow! Meow! Meow!"

"Oh, don't cry," said Sam.

Sam showed Katie the kitten a big, red balloon he had found.

"You can have fun playing with this, instead," smiled Sam.

But as Katie pounced on the balloon, it burst. BANG! The loud noise made Katie jump!

"Meow! Meow!" said Katie. "I think I have played enough games for one day."

Katie drank her milk and washed her paws. Then she curled up beside her friend, Sam.

"Sweet dreams, little kitten," said Sam, as Katie went to sleep.

Penny the Pony

All the animals had gathered to watch Penny the pony and Harry Hare race around the field.

There was a special prize of a big bag of carrots for the winner!

Faster! Faster! cheered their friends, as Penny and Harry began the race.

It was a very close race, but Penny won by the tip of her nose!

...19...

Baby Rabbit was bouncing up and down on the fence, cheering his friends on, when he slipped and fell.

"Baby Rabbit has bumped his head! We must fetch Doctor Dog straight away," said Mother Rabbit.

"I will find him," said Penny.

Without looking back, Penny the pony ran towards the farm.

I must run faster than I have ever run before! thought Penny.

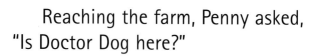

Reaching the farm, Penny asked, "Is Doctor Dog here?"

"Moo! Moo!" replied Daisy the cow. "Doctor Dog is not here, I'm afraid. Why don't you try Billy Bear's house? Perhaps Doctor Dog is visiting him."

"Thank you, I will," said Penny.

Without looking back, Penny ran off as fast as she could.

I must run faster than I have ever run before! thought Penny.

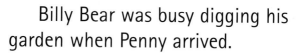

Billy Bear was busy digging his garden when Penny arrived.

"Is Doctor Dog here with you?" asked Penny.

"No, I haven't seen him all day," said Billy Bear. "Why don't you go to the wood and find Ollie Owl? He knows everything."

Without looking back, Penny ran off as fast as she could.

I must run faster than I have ever run before! thought Penny.

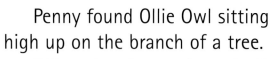

Penny found Ollie Owl sitting high up on the branch of a tree.

Ollie, who always sleeps in the daytime, opened one eye when he heard Penny running towards him.

"Can you tell me where to find Doctor Dog?" asked Penny.

"He has gone for a walk in the wood," said Ollie.

Without looking back, Penny ran off as fast as she could.

I must run faster than I have ever run before! thought Penny.

Jumping over dead branches and piles of leaves, Penny soon caught up with Doctor Dog.

"Baby Rabbit has fallen and bumped his head!" said Penny. "Please can you help him?"
"Of course!" said Doctor Dog as he jumped on Penny's back.

Without looking back, Penny galloped towards the field as fast as she could.
I must run faster than I have ever run before! thought Penny.

Jumping down from Penny's back, Doctor Dog looked at Baby Rabbit's head.

"There, you are all better now," smiled Doctor Dog, as he wrapped a bandage around Baby Rabbit's head.

"Thank you for your help, Doctor Dog and Penny the pony," said Mother Rabbit.

But without looking back, Penny had already gone off to eat some of her juicy carrots!

Three Little Ducklings

One morning, just as he was drinking his tea, Billy Bear's telephone rang. It was Dilly Duck.

"You are invited to the ducklings' surprise birthday party on Saturday," said Dilly. "Will you call Paddy the dog and ask him to come, too?"

"I love surprise birthday parties!" said Billy. "I will call Paddy now."

Brrriiing! Brrriiing! Paddy the dog heard his telephone ringing.

"Hello," said Paddy, picking up the receiver.

"Hello, Paddy," said Billy Bear. "Dilly Duck has invited you to a surprise birthday party for the ducklings on Saturday. Will you please call Hoppy Rabbit and ask him to come too?"

"I love surprise birthday parties!" said Paddy. "I will call Hoppy now."

Brrriiing! Brrriiing! Hoppy Rabbit heard his telephone ringing.

"Hello," said Hoppy, picking up the receiver.

"Hello, Hoppy," said Paddy. "Dilly Duck has invited you to a surprise birthday party for the ducklings on Saturday. Will you call Sammy Squirrel and ask him to come too?"

"I love surprise birthday parties!" said Hoppy. "I will call Sammy now."

Brrriiing! Brrriiing! Sammy Squirrel's telephone rang and rang and rang, but no-one answered.

"Oh dear," sighed Hoppy Rabbit. "I wonder why Sammy is not answering his telephone?"

Sammy Squirrel was outside in his garden, busily collecting nuts for winter, and did not hear his telephone ringing.

Brrriiing! Brrriiing!

Hoppy Rabbit hopped all the way to Sammy Squirrel's house to tell him about the surprise party that was being given for the ducklings.

"There you are!" said Hoppy, finding Sammy in his garden.

Just then, Sammy's phone rang again, Brrriiing! Brrriiing!

"Your telephone is ringing again, Sammy," said Hoppy.

"Will you answer it for me?" said Sammy. "I am busy collecting nuts."

Hoppy Rabbit answered the telephone. It was Molly Mouse calling Sammy to have a chat.

"Sammy is busy collecting nuts," said Hoppy. Then he told Molly about the surprise party for the ducklings on Saturday.

"What time does it start?" asked Molly, excitedly.

"Three o'clock," said Hoppy. "Don't be late."

"I won't," said Molly. "Goodbye."

At last the day of the party arrived. What a wonderful surprise the ducklings had when they saw all their friends.

Brrriiing! Brrriiing! Just as the birthday party was about to begin, the telephone rang. Dilly Duck answered the call.

"I am on my way!" said Grandma Duck, at the other end of the line.

When Grandma arrived with the cake, everyone sang happy birthday to the ducklings.

Cassie the Cow

Cassie the cow could not find her calf.
"Moo! Moo! Moo!" called Cassie.
But there was no answer.

Cassie decided to search for her calf. He has probably wandered off to play with his friends on the farm, Cassie thought to herself.

As she trotted across a field, Cassie passed Farmer Brown on his red tractor.

Then Cassie saw Paddy the dog. He was sitting in a corner, happily chewing on a big pile of bones.

"Paddy, have you seen my little calf?" asked Cassie.

"No, I have not seen him at all today," said Paddy.

Cassie was very upset. "Moo! Moo!" she called, as she walked towards the duck pond. "I wonder where my baby has gone?"

At the pond, Mother Duck and her ducklings were making a lot of noise. "Quack! Quack!" they said.

Cassie could see that her calf was not there.

"Moo! Moo! Where are you, little calf?" called Cassie.

"Quack! Quack!" called Mother Duck. "We have not seen your calf at all today, Cassie."

"Quack! Quack! Perhaps he is playing with the piglets in their pig sty," said the ducklings.

Cassie the cow trotted down to the pig sty, where the piglets were happily squealing as they played and rolled around in the mud.

Cassie could see that her calf was not there.

Quickly turning round, Cassie hurried towards the farmyard.

"Moo! Moo! Where are you, little calf?" called Cassie. "It is getting very late, you know."

But there was still no reply.

Cassie saw Mother Hen in the farmyard. She was busy taking care of her six fluffy chicks.

"Have you seen my calf?" asked Cassie, worriedly.

"Cluck! Cluck! No, I have not," said Mother Hen. "Perhaps he has gone to play in the meadow?"

As she made her way towards the meadow, Cassie called for her calf. "Moo! Moo! Where are you?"

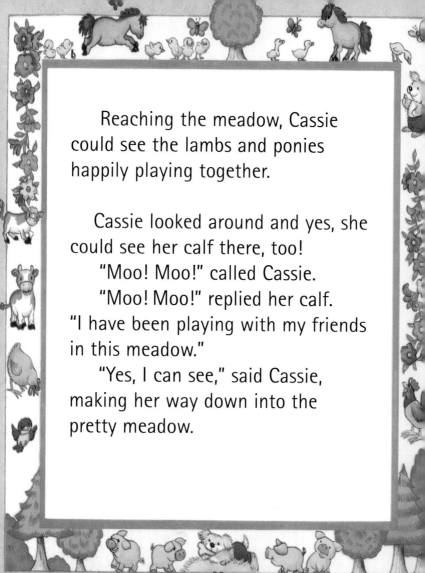

Reaching the meadow, Cassie
could see the lambs and ponies
happily playing together.

Cassie looked around and yes, she
could see her calf there, too!
"Moo! Moo!" called Cassie.
"Moo! Moo!" replied her calf.
"I have been playing with my friends
in this meadow."
"Yes, I can see," said Cassie,
making her way down into the
pretty meadow.

"In future, you must always tell me where you are going, then I won't worry," said Cassie, giving her calf a big, wet lick.

"I will," promised the calf. "Now can I play with my friends for just a little while longer?"

"You can play with them again tomorrow," promised Cassie. "Now it is time for you to come home."

"See you tomorrow!" the calf called to his friends, as his mummy led him safely home.

Little Lost Chick

Paddy the dog and his friends were playing in the wood one day, when they found a baby chick.

"Are you lost, little chick?" asked Billy Bear.

The baby chick nodded his head. "Cheep! Cheep!" he sobbed. "I want my mummy!"

"I expect you do," smiled Paddy. "Now dry your tears and we will help you to find your mummy."

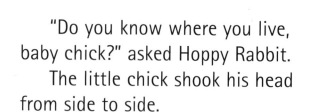

"Do you know where you live, baby chick?" asked Hoppy Rabbit.

The little chick shook his head from side to side.

"Cheep! Cheep!" cried the chick, louder and louder. "I-I do not remember where I live. I will never find my mummy again!"

"Yes, you will," said Dilly Duck, giving the little chick a hug. "My friends and I will help you to search until we find your mummy. Just you wait and see."

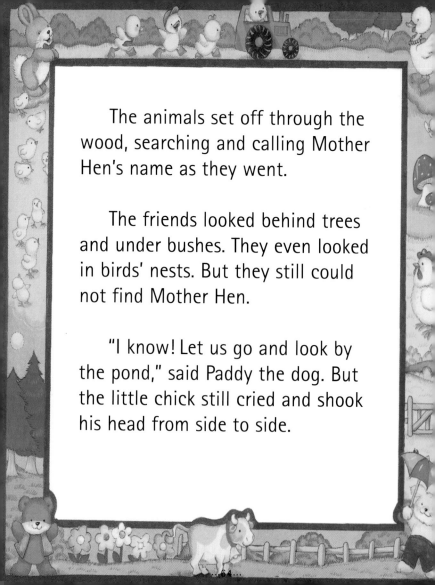

The animals set off through the wood, searching and calling Mother Hen's name as they went.

The friends looked behind trees and under bushes. They even looked in birds' nests. But they still could not find Mother Hen.

"I know! Let us go and look by the pond," said Paddy the dog. But the little chick still cried and shook his head from side to side.

"Have you seen Mother Hen?" Dilly Duck asked her ducklings, when the friends reached the pond.

"Yes, Mother Hen is at the farm," said the ducklings.

Smiling, the little chick nodded his head up and down and said, "Cheep! Cheep! Now I know where my mother is, I am happy again!"

"What are we waiting for?" laughed the other animals. "Let us all go to the farm."

Hoppy Rabbit knew the quickest way to the farm. "Everyone follow me!" he called, as Teddy, Dilly Duck and Billy Bear skipped down a winding path.

"Hey, do not forget me!" chirped the little chick, running to catch up with the others.

Hoppy led the friends around trees and bushes, up and over a hill, across the meadow, and through an open gate.

"We are nearly there now," said Hoppy. "Look! There is Gertrude the cow in the meadow."

"Cheep! Cheep!" said the chick, who knew he didn't have far to go.

"Hurry along there, little chick," mooed Gertrude the cow. "Mother Hen has been calling you. It is time for you to go to sleep."

"Just a short way to go," said Hoppy Rabbit.

"Come on, little chick. Let me carry you," said Teddy.

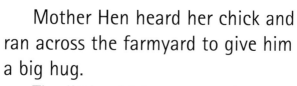

Mother Hen heard her chick and ran across the farmyard to give him a big hug.

The little chick was very happy to be safely home with all his brothers and sisters again.

"Thank you for bringing my chick home," Mother Hen told Hoppy Rabbit and his friends.

"We didn't mind at all," smiled Hoppy. "Your little chicks can come and play with me and my friends whenever they want to."

A New Friend

Bert the bear lived in a lovely old caravan. His horse, Harriet, pulled the caravan along winding country lanes, up and over hills, and from village to village.

Every day, Bert and Harriet rode through the countryside. Then every evening, Bert found a field where Harriet could rest and eat her dinner. At night they went to sleep under the stars.

Late one evening, as Bert fetched Harriet's bucket from under the caravan, he heard a strange noise. It was coming from inside Harriet's bucket!

Bert got down on his knees and listened carefully. He heard a croaky little voice say, "Go away! Croak! Croak! Leave me alone..."

Whatever could it be?

Harriet heard the voice, too. Then she saw a little frog sitting in her bucket!

"What a cheek! Tip it out," said Harriet. "I don't want a frog in my bucket!"

"Don't worry. I will take the frog back to the stream," said Bert.

"Please don't do that," said the frog. "Take me with you on your travels. I will not be any trouble, I promise! Croak! Croak!"

"You cannot live in my bucket," Harriet told the frog.

"Then we will buy another one," said Bert.

"Oh, all right!" said Harriet.

The little frog jumped on to the grass and began spinning round with excitement. "My name is Dizzy," he said, happily.

Harriet shook her head. "I have always thought frogs were silly," she said, trying not to laugh.

A Bucket for Dizzy

The next morning, Bert and Harriet set off with Dizzy sitting in Harriet's bucket. It was very hot.

Bert the bear made a paper hat for Harriet, to help keep the sun off her head.

"Do you think my hat looks silly?" asked Harriet.

"Yes," giggled Dizzy. But Harriet did not care. She was very hot.

After a while, Harriet stopped to have a drink from her bucket.

"You won't drink all the water, will you?" asked Dizzy.

"This water is for drinking, not for sitting in!" said Harriet.

"But I will shrivel up without water," said Dizzy.

Bert took a cupful of water from the bucket and said, "Hop in there, Dizzy. Then Harriet has enough water to drink, and you have enough water to keep wet."

Harriet drank the rest of her water, then set off again.

As they clip-clopped along the winding roads, Dizzy sat in the cup, next to Bert.

But there was not enough water in the cup to keep Dizzy wet. Soon, the sun started to feel even hotter.

Harriet's feet began to drag.

"We will have to find some more water soon," said Bert.

Suddenly, Dizzy sniffed the air. "Bring the bucket and follow me!" he called to Bert. "I will find some water for you."

Dizzy jumped out of the cup and on to the road. Bert tried to follow Dizzy, but the little frog was too quick.

Dizzy hopped faster and faster. At last he saw a stream. "Croak!" he called, diving in.

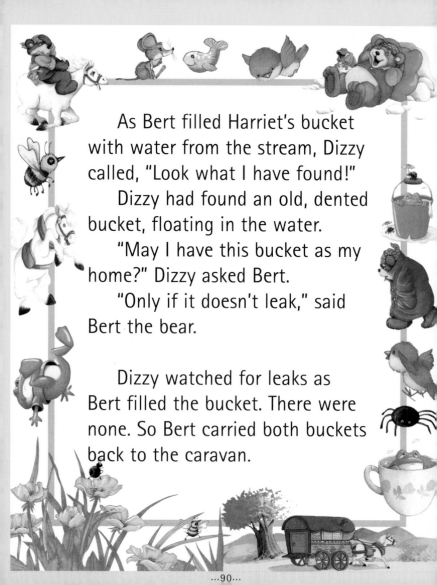

As Bert filled Harriet's bucket with water from the stream, Dizzy called, "Look what I have found!"

Dizzy had found an old, dented bucket, floating in the water.

"May I have this bucket as my home?" Dizzy asked Bert.

"Only if it doesn't leak," said Bert the bear.

Dizzy watched for leaks as Bert filled the bucket. There were none. So Bert carried both buckets back to the caravan.

"What have you got there?" asked Harriet. "And where is that little frog?"

"Here!" said Dizzy, popping his head out of the bucket he had found. "Now I have my very own bucket to sit in!"

"That's a relief," said Harriet.

When Bert went back to the stream to fill her bucket again, Harriet said to Dizzy, "You are not so bad for a frog, I suppose!"

Visitors

Harriet was not happy. She could see for miles ahead, and she did not like to see how far she had to travel. Then Harriet saw a cave.

I do not like caves, thought Harriet, shaking her head.

But when Bert saw the cave, he took Dizzy from his bucket and said, "Let us go and explore."

"I am not going into a cave," said Harriet, shaking her head.

As Bert carried Dizzy and a lantern into the dark cave, Dizzy made funny shapes on the walls with his own shadow.

Suddenly, Dizzy heard Harriet calling. Bert and Dizzy hurried outside to find Harriet staring up at the sky.

"It's a...a...," was all Harriet could manage to say.

"Quickly! Into the cave," said Bert, pulling Harriet inside, too.

"What is it?" asked Dizzy, his voice trembling with fear.

"I think it is a flying saucer!" whispered Bert.

Harriet did not say a word. She just kept her eyes tightly closed!

"What are we going to do?" asked Dizzy.

"We must stay hidden and watch," said Bert. "Now please be quiet and stop asking questions!"

Suddenly, Bert, Dizzy and Harriet heard a strange noise. A flying saucer had landed on a nearby hill!

Dizzy jumped into the safety of Bert's pocket.

Opening her eyes, Harriet saw lots of little green figures jumping from the flying saucer.

"What are they doing?" asked Dizzy, as Harriet quickly closed her eyes again.

"They are having a picnic," said Bert, smiling.

"You will be telling me they are picking daisies next!" said Harriet.

"They are!" said Bert.

"How dare they!" said Harriet.

Frightened by Harriet's voice, the little green figures ran back to their flying saucer, which took off.

"What a strange dream I have just had," said Harriet, as she opened her eyes. "I dreamt I saw a flying saucer!"

The Birthday Party

That night, Bert, Harriet and Dizzy stopped to rest by a stream. Bert tipped Dizzy out of his bucket and into the stream. Then he gave Harriet her dinner.

A little later, Bert looked for his lantern, but he could not find it. He had left it in the cave.

"I put it on the ground when we went into the cave, and I forgot to pick it up," he said.

"I suppose I will have to stand in the dark," said Harriet.

"You always do stand in the dark, silly horse!" said Dizzy, as he hopped over and sat beside Bert on the caravan steps.

A short time later, Bert heard Harriet calling him.

"What is wrong?" asked Bert, going over to Harriet.

"There is something moving in the water," said Harriet.

Bert could see shapes coming out of the water.

"What are they?" asked Harriet.

Dizzy bounced up and down. "They are frogs!" he laughed.

"Well, go and see what they want," said Harriet.

Dizzy hopped away. Then Harriet and Bert heard some loud croaking noises!

"Bert! Save Dizzy!" gasped Harriet. "He needs our help!"

"I don't need saving!" called Dizzy, hopping back to his friends. "This is a birthday party. Grandpa Bullfrog is one hundred bullfrog years old today. We are all invited."

"I think we should stay here and watch the party," Bert told Harriet. "Frogs are very small, and we might tread on one of them if we join in."

So Bert and Harriet watched as the frogs danced and sang songs.

It was such a good party that Harriet even sang a few songs with her new frog friends.

"That was the best birthday party I have ever been to," said Dizzy, giving a big, big yawn.

"We will go back and fetch the lantern tomorrow," said Bert. "Let's get some sleep now, before the birds start to sing!"

Early in the morning, the frogs began their journey home.

New Shoes for Harriet

Harriet's feet were hurting her. "I need some new shoes!" she said, rather grumpily.

"Horses do not wear shoes!" said Dizzy.

"Oh, yes they do," said Bert, showing Dizzy the metal shoes nailed to Harriet's feet.

Harriet looked so sad, that Bert decided to take her to a blacksmith straight away.

Leaving the caravan behind, Dizzy sat on Bert's shoulder as he walked along beside Harriet.

At the blacksmith's, Dizzy watched as nails were hammered into Harriet's hooves.

"Does it hurt very much?" Dizzy asked Harriet.

"Of course not!" said Harriet.

"Ooh, poor Harriet!" said Dizzy, every time the hammer hit a nail.

Harriet felt much better when her old shoes had been replaced.

As she walked along, Harriet let Bert ride on her back.

A little later, as Harriet trotted along, Bert whispered to Dizzy, "I think Harriet is going the wrong way for our caravan."

"Then you must stop her before we get completely lost," said Dizzy.

Bert gently pulled Harriet's mane and she stopped.

"What is wrong?" asked Harriet.

"We are going the wrong way," called Dizzy.

Harriet wandered up lanes and across fields, but they could not find the caravan. Soon it began to get dark.

Suddenly, Harriet slipped down a steep grassy bank! Bert flew over her head and SPLASH!

"Bert, where are you?" called Harriet, worriedly.

The moon came out from behind a cloud and Harriet saw Bert. He was sitting in the middle of a pond, covered in weeds.

"Where is Dizzy?" asked Bert. Dizzy was sitting on Bert's head.

"I am up here," said Dizzy, sliding down into Bert's shirt.

"Ooh, you are tickling me!" laughed Bert.

The more Dizzy wriggled about, the more he tickled Bert, and the more Bert laughed.

At last, Bert pulled Dizzy out of his shirt. By now, Dizzy and even Harriet were laughing, too.

Bert pushed Harriet up the grassy slope, and there, in front of them, was the caravan.

"Of course, I knew it was there all the time," said Harriet.

Bert and Dizzy just smiled.

Mud

It was a very windy day and Harriet was not at all happy. She did not like the way the road twisted and turned.

"Why can't it be straight, like other roads?" she said. "I want to walk in a straight line."

Bert climbed down from the caravan and walked beside Harriet. "Stop complaining," he said.

I will show them, Harriet thought to herself.

Before Bert had time to stop her, Harriet stepped off the road and on to the muddy grass, pulling the caravan with her.

Dizzy's bucket made a splish-splosh sound.

"Stop it, Harriet!" called Bert, as he tried to pull the horse back. "Stop it at once!"

As Harriet stopped, Dizzy said, "Look at her feet!"

Bert looked down to see Harriet's feet sinking in the mud.

"Help me!" cried Harriet.

But as soon as Bert pulled one of Harriet's legs free, another one sank into the mud!

"There is no time to lose! We must unhitch Harriet from the caravan," said Dizzy.

Bert unhitched Harriet from the caravan, and she managed to pull herself out of the mud and back on to the road.

Bert sadly watched as the caravan then began to sink.

"I will get some help," said Dizzy, hopping away.

Meanwhile, Bert grabbed the rope at the back of the caravan, and Harriet held on to him so that he did not fall into the mud.

At last, Dizzy returned with a crowd of frogs. The frogs were too light to sink into the mud.

Bert cut some heather and the frogs pulled it on to the mud and around the caravan's wheels.

Bert tied the rope to Harriet and she slowly dragged the caravan over the carpet of heather and back to the road.

"Three cheers for the frogs!" said Bert. "Hip, hip, hooray!"

Atishoo!

Bert was lying in the sun, Harriet was busy eating grass, and Dizzy was exploring.

Suddenly, Bert heard, "Atishoo!"

"What was that?" asked Bert.

"It was me... aaatishoo!" said Dizzy. "Aaatishoo!"

"Are you getting a cold?" asked Bert, worriedly.

"Frogs do not get colds!" said Dizzy. "Atishoo! Atishoo!"

"What is the matter with Dizzy?" asked Harriet.

"What do you think! Atishoo! Atishoo! Atishoo!" said Dizzy.

Bert picked Dizzy up and carried him into the caravan.

"Perhaps the sun is making you sneeze," said Bert, putting Dizzy on the table.

Just as Dizzy thought the sneezing had stopped, "Atishoo!" he began sneezing again.

The last sneeze was so strong, that it threw Dizzy backwards, into a big bag of flour!

Covered in flour, Dizzy could not see or hear a thing.

Bert could not stop laughing at the funny sight.

"Help! Atishoo! Help! Help!" said Dizzy, jumping out of the caravan.

Bert was still laughing as Dizzy stumbled around, searching for his bucket of water.

"Atishoo!" said Dizzy. "Where is my bucket?"

Bert tried to tell Dizzy, but he was laughing too much.

Dizzy bounced towards Harriet, who was surprised to see a white shape hopping around her legs.

As Harriet looked down to take a closer look, the white shape bounced, and hit her on the nose!

"Yikes!" cried Harriet.

Harriet began to jump and leap about. "Help me, Bert!" she called.

But Bert was laughing even more at the funny sight.

Still unable to see where he was going, Dizzy hopped away as fast as he could.

Bert tried to grab hold of Harriet's tail to stop her jumping around, but he could not catch her.

Lying on the grass, Bert laughed until tears rolled down his face.

"Why is Harriet jumping about like that?" said a voice in Bert's ear. It was Dizzy. He was still sneezing, but he had wiped the flour from his eyes and ears.

As Bert explained to Dizzy what had happened, Harriet galloped towards them.

Dizzy and Bert quickly jumped for safety. Dizzy ran under a big fence, and Bert leaped over it.

"Why am I running around?" asked Harriet, looking confused.

Before Bert had time to answer, Dizzy sneezed.

"Why doesn't Dizzy wipe the pollen off his nose?" asked Harriet.

Bert looked at Dizzy's nose. It was yellow, like buttercup pollen.

"Pollen always makes frogs sneeze," said Harriet.

"I didn't know that," said Bert.

Neither did Harriet. She had made it up!

Bert found a small paintbrush
and used it to clean Dizzy's nose.
The brush tickled and made Dizzy
laugh. But at least he was not
sneezing anymore.

"That will teach you not to put
your nose into buttercups," said
Harriet. "Now, remind me why
I was running about like that?"
Dizzy did not dare tell Harriet
the truth. The less she knew about
this adventure, the better!

Waves

"There is the sea," said Bert, pointing into the distance.

"Can we go closer?" asked Harriet.

"We can go right to the very edge," said Bert.

Luckily, Dizzy was asleep in his bucket, otherwise he would have had a few questions to ask, too.

The friends were right beside the sea before Dizzy woke up.

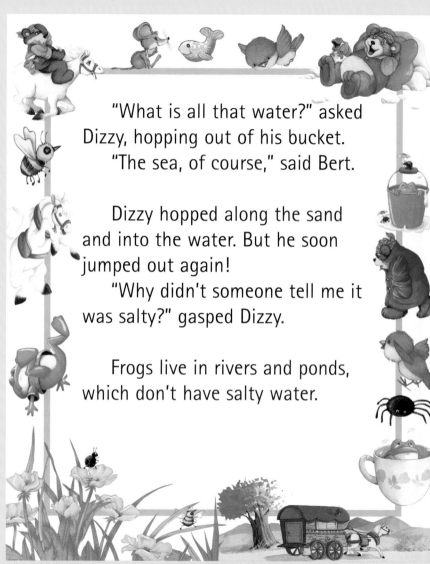

"What is all that water?" asked Dizzy, hopping out of his bucket.

"The sea, of course," said Bert.

Dizzy hopped along the sand and into the water. But he soon jumped out again!

"Why didn't someone tell me it was salty?" gasped Dizzy.

Frogs live in rivers and ponds, which don't have salty water.

Harriet wanted to take a closer look at the sea.

"You won't like it," warned Dizzy. "Come away!"

But Harriet did like the sea. She galloped along the beach, through the frothy waves. Bert had never seen Harriet so happy.

Later, Harriet told Bert that the sea had made her feel young again.

"Now I understand why you like water so much," Harriet told Dizzy.

"Not the salty kind," said Dizzy.

"Oh, well," said Harriet. "Horses always have had more sense than frogs!"

Then she plodded off happily while Dizzy settled into his bucket of water that did not have a trace of salt in it.